Harry and His Bucket Full of Dinosaurs

I'm Not Scared of Monsters!

Based on the original stories created by
Ian Whybrow and Adrian Reynolds
Illustrated by Art Mawhinney

PUFFIN BOOKS
Published by the Penguin Group: London, New York,
Australia, Canada, India, Ireland, New Zealand and South Africa
Penguin Books Ltd, Registered Offices: 80 Strand, London WC2R 0RL, England

puffinbooks.com

First published 2007
1 3 5 7 9 10 8 6 4 2

Made and printed in China
ISBN: 978–0–141–50138–3

It was late at night. Harry was supposed to be asleep.
Instead he took his torch under his covers and drew a monster!

"Aaagh!" shouted Harry when his mother caught him.

"Time to go to sleep, Harry," she said.

Harry groaned.

"Hmm . . . Scary drawing," said his mother as she looked at his
monster. "I hope you don't have nightmares."

Once he fell asleep, Harry did have a nightmare.
He dreamed his monster was chasing him!
"Aaaagh!" shouted Harry.

Harry's shout woke
up his dinosaur friends.
"It sounds like
Harry's in big trouble!"
said Trike.

"Harry needs us,"
said Taury. "Follow me!"
Taury and the other
dinosaurs charged
out of the bucket to
rescue Harry.

But the dinosaurs couldn't find a monster in Harry's room.

"Let's go to sleep," said Pterence.

"What if the monster comes back?" said Harry.

"We could go where the monster can't find us,"
suggested Steggy.

"I know!" said Harry. "Let's go to Dino World!"

"Good thinking, Harry!" said Sid.

"You'll be safe there!" agreed Taury.

"One, two, three! Jump, Harry!" shouted the dinosaurs.

Harry leaped into the bucket.

"I'm on my way to Dino World!"

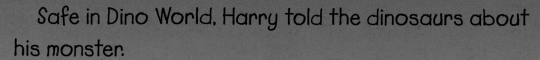

Safe in Dino World, Harry told the dinosaurs about
his monster.

"It has scary hairy fur," Harry began.

"Ooooh," said the dinosaurs.

"And huge teeth and long, sharp claws," Harry continued.

"Ooooh," said the dinosaurs.

"And it has a ferocious roar!"

Just then, a ferocious roar rang out all over
Dino World: "Yaaagh!"
   "Yeah!" said Harry. "His roar was just like that."
   Then Harry realized what had happened.
   The monster had followed him to Dino World!
   "Aaagh!" Harry shouted.
   The monster towered over Harry and the dinosaurs!
And he was just as terrible, horrible and scary as
            Harry had said. His big monster foot almost
            stomped right on Harry!

But Taury quickly came to his rescue. He put Harry on his shoulders and ran as fast as he could.

"You're safe with me, Harry," said Taury as he ran.

"What if that monster catches up?" said Harry.

"It won't," said Taury. "I'm way too fast."

"What if he grows huge legs?" asked Harry.

Just as Harry said this, the monster's legs grew huge and he began catching up with Harry and Taury!

"Faster, Taury, faster," cried Harry.
"Sorry, Harry," said Taury, out of breath, "can't go faster, getting tired . . ."

"Look, Taury!" cried Harry. "The Dino Mobile!"
Taury and Harry hopped in the Dino Mobile. They zipped away from the monster just in time.
"We did it!" said Harry. "We're safe from the monster."

But Taury could see that Harry still looked worried.

"What's the matter, Harry?" he asked.

"What if the monster goes after the others?" asked Harry.

Just as Harry said this, the monster turned right round and went after the others.

"NOOOO!" cried Harry.

Harry and Taury found the other dinosaurs running as fast as they could away from the monster.

"Follow us to Pepper Rock," yelled Taury. "We'll be safe there."

"Wait for me!" cried Pterence, who had fallen behind.

Harry and the dinosaurs gathered inside the cave in
Pepper Rock.

"We made it," said Taury.

"Everyone's safe," said Harry.

"Everyone except Pterence," said Trike.

"Where is Pterence?" asked Sid.

"He's out there with that monster!" said Taury.

Outside the cave, Pterence was all alone with the angry monster.

The monster snarled at Pterence and swatted at him with his giant furry hand.

Pterence shook with fear.

"I won't let that monster
scare Pterence!" said Harry.
"I've got to save him."
   "Be careful, Harry,"
said Patsy.

   Harry marched outside
the cave. The monster was
as scary as ever.
   But Harry was brave.
   "Hey, monster," he yelled.
"You leave Pterence alone!"

"You're not so big!" said Harry.

The monster shrank.

"Your teeth aren't huge and your claws aren't so long and sharp."

The monster's teeth became small and his claws became short and round.

"Your fur isn't very scary either," said Harry. "Especially when it has polka dots and stripes!"

The monster's fur changed just the way Harry said.

"Good monster!" said Harry with a smile. The monster wasn't one bit scary any more.

Harry invited the little monster to have roasted marshmallows with him and his dinosaur friends.

"No wonder Harry could change the monster," said Sid, "he's the one who imagined it in the first place!"

But soon Harry felt sleepy.

"I think it's time to go to bed," said Harry.

Harry climbed into his very own bed.
"Goodnight, everyone," said Harry.
"We'll watch over you while you're sleeping," said Taury,
"No thanks," said Harry. "I'm not scared of
monsters any more."

And he really truly wasn't.